About the Author

Flora writes and illustrates books for children helping them to stay positive and find the happiness and adventure in life. Flora lives in the sunny South of England and has had a passion for writing stories and illustrating them for many years. When she was only six years old her dad would write a story and Flora would illustrate it and make it into a little book. The passion grew and this is how *The Dragon Who Lost His Wings* was born. Flora is still studying illustration and graphic design along with creating more amazing adventures for children.

The Dragon Who Lost His Wings

Flora

The Dragon Who Lost His Wings

Nightingale Books

NIGHTINGALE PAPERBACK

© Copyright 2021
Flora

A CIP catalogue record for this title is
available from the British Library.
ISBN 978-1-83875-391-7

Nightingale Books is an imprint of
Pegasus Elliot MacKenzie Publishers Ltd.

www.pegasuspublishers.com

First Published in 2021

Nightingale Books
Sheraton House Castle Park
Cambridge England

Printed & Bound in Great Britain

Dedication

This book is dedicated to my father who has never stopped supporting me no matter what life has thrown at us. In memory of writing stories together on the kitchen side when I was six.

Acknowledgements

Thank you to Jon Leftley, my graphics teacher, who supported me in my dreams. To Itchen College for helping me learn and grow. To Steph Cooke for believing in me when I didn't.

I WAS A DRAGON THAT WAS SO SAD
AS I HAD LOST MY WINGS AND IT MADE ME FEEL BAD.

I LOOKED IN THE FOREST AND NOTHING WAS THERE,
I EVEN ASKED THE BIG FURRY BEAR.

"TRY BY THE LAKE," THE BEAR DID SAY.
"I HOPE THEY'RE THERE, IT WILL MAKE MY DAY."

OFF TO THE LAKE I DID SCURRY,
RUNNING FAST AS I WAS IN A HURRY.

I GOT TO THE LAKE AND IT WAS BIG AND BLUE,
BUT WHERE TO LOOK, I HAD NO CLUE.

AROUND THE EDGE, BEHIND A ROCK,
BUT ALL I FOUND WAS AN OLD SMELLY SOCK.

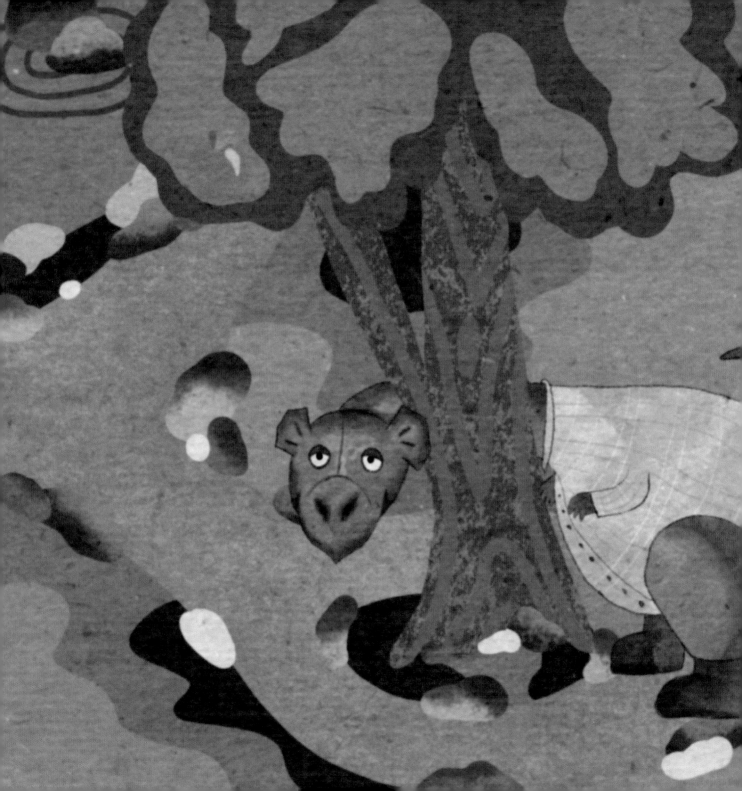

I THOUGHT, 'OH NO, WHERE CAN MY WINGS BE?'
I KEEP LOOKING BEHIND EVERY TREE.

I SAT BY THE LAKE ON THE GROUND,
I LOOKED INTO THE WATER AND GUESS WHAT I FOUND.

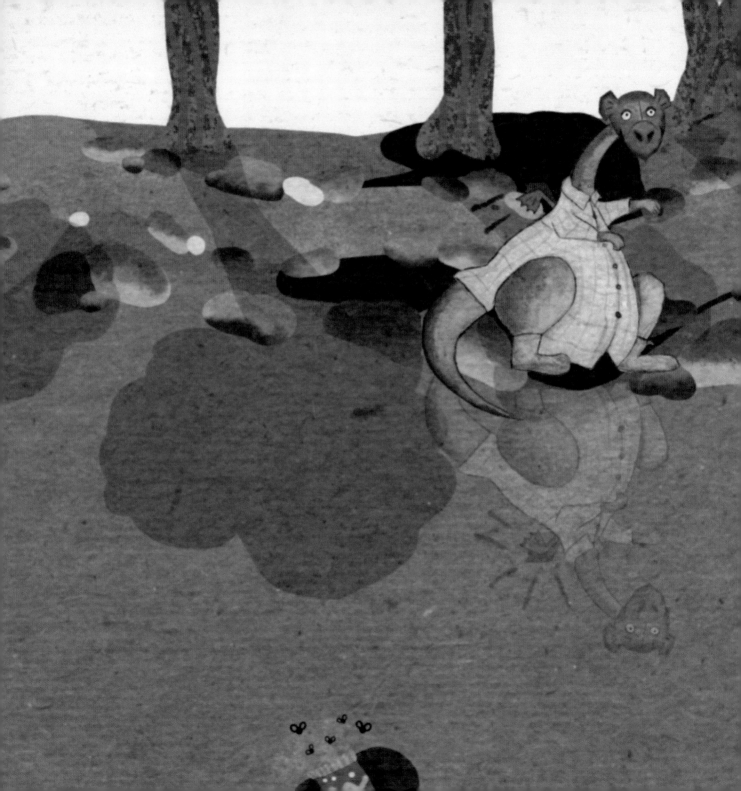

MY REFLECTION SHOWED ME HOW SILLY I CAN BE,
AS MY WINGS WERE THERE ALREADY SAT ON ME.

BONUS PAGE

Printed in Great Britain
by Amazon